Bedtime Blessings

Written and illustrated by
Marianne Richmond

sourcebooks
jabberwocky

Copyright © 2016 by Marianne Richmond
Cover and internal design © 2016 by Sourcebooks, Inc.
Cover and internal illustrations © Marianne Richmond
Cover design by Brittany Vibbert/Sourcebooks, Inc.

Published by Sourcebooks Jabberwocky, an imprint of Sourcebooks, Inc.
P.O. Box 4410, Naperville, Illinois 60567-4410
(630) 961-3900
Fax: (630) 961-2168
www.sourcebooks.com

Library of Congress Cataloging-in-Publication data is on file with the publisher.

Source of Production: Worzalla, Stevens Point, WI
Date of Production: July 2016
Run Number: 5007071

Printed and bound in the United States of America.
WOZ 10 9 8 7 6 5 4 3 2 1

Thanks, God, for everything.

Dear God,

It's the end of the day
> and time for my prayer

to say **thanks for your blessings**
> and heavenly care.

Thank you for my family

both here and far away

who give me **so much love**

by what they do and say.

Thank you, too, for all we have,
      our home and food and clothes,

and how we know **you're with us**

wherever we may go.

Thank you for my body
growing healthy, tall, and strong

and for my brain that knows a lot
from learning **all day long.**

Thank you for my playmates
who like to laugh and run,

and for my favorite toys and books
that *fill our day with fun.*

Thank _you_ for the world outside
with flowers, lakes, and trees,

and for the birds and butterflies
who decorate the breeze.

Thank you for my furry friends,
whose faces I adore,
and how they make me laugh aloud
whenever we explore.

Thank you, God, for everything,
my blessings big and small.

I pray that others get to know

your kindness most of all.

Bless the ones I love so much.
May good things come their way.

Help them see these *gifts from you*
through each and every day.

Bless the choices that I make
so I can honor you.

Help me show *you're in my heart*
through all I say and do.

Bless the friends we know and love
who are feeling sick or sad.

Let them know *you're always there*
through both the good and bad.

Bless the great big world you made
and give us each day new.

Help us to be full of thanks,
for we belong to you.

My eyes are getting sleepy now.
The stars are bright above.
Guide me into peaceful dreams

held safely in your love.

And when I wake tomorrow,
I'll be ready once again
to enjoy *your many blessings.*

Good night.
Thank you.
Amen.

ABOUT THE AUTHOR

Beloved author and illustrator Marianne Richmond has touched the lives of millions for nearly two decades through her award-winning books and gift products that offer meaningful ways to connect with the people and moments that matter.